Stickybeak

Story by Hazel Edwards
Illustrations by Rosemary Wilson

For a free color catalog describing Gareth Steven's list of high-quality children's
books, call 1-800-341-3569 (USA) or 1-800-461-9120 (Canada).

Library of Congress Cataloging-in-Publication Data

Edwards, Hazel.
Stickybeak.

Summary: A child describes the adventuresome weekend spent caring for the class's pet duck.
[1. Ducks—Fiction] I. Wilson, Rosemary, ill. II. Title. PZ7.E2545St   1988   [E] 88-42915 ISBN 1-55532-932-2

North American edition first published in 1989 by **Gareth Stevens Children's Books**
1555 North RiverCenter Drive, Suite 201, Milwaukee, Wisconsin 53212, USA

US edition copyright © 1989. Text copyright © Hazel Edwards, 1986. Illustrations copyright
© Rosemary Wilson, 1986. First published in Australia by Nelson Publishers.

Printed in the United States of America

3 4 5 6 7 8 9 97 96 95 94 93 92

Gareth Stevens Children's Books
MILWAUKEE

Just for this weekend, Stickybeak is my pet.
From Monday to Friday, he lives in a box at school.

Everyone at school talks a lot.
So does Stickybeak.
"Quack! Quack! Quack!"

We looked after three duck eggs.
But only one duck grew.
It thought we were its parents.

The class voted for its name.
    Danny had 2 votes.
    Fluffy had 6 votes.
    Donald had 20 votes.

But Ms. Pappas said, "Donald is a cartoon duck.
Our duck is different."

So we changed our minds.
We called him Stickybeak!

On Friday, it was my turn.
I took Stickybeak home in a box.
We put the seat belt around him.

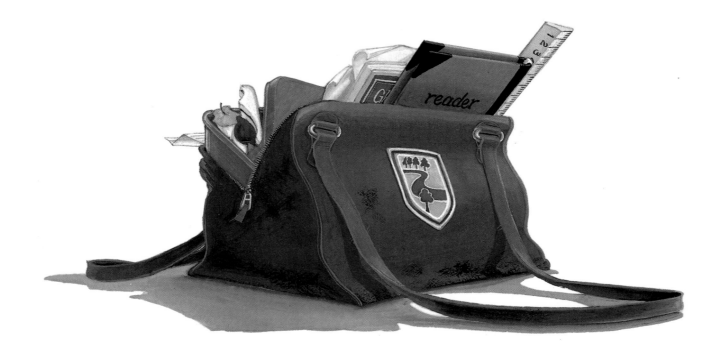

"What do ducks eat?" Mom asked.
She doesn't like pets very much.
"Corn flakes," I said.
"Quack! Quack! Quack!" said Stickybeak.

At the supermarket, frozen duck was on SPECIAL.
"Not this weekend, I guess," Mom said.

At home, Stickybeak quacked all the time.
And he messed up his box too.

After dinner, I put fresh newspaper and water in his box.

"Where's my newspaper?" asked Mom.
"I want to read the news."

"Sorry, Mom. Stickybeak's using it."

Mom didn't like it much
when I gave Stickybeak a swim in our bathtub.

"Snails have been nibbling on my flowers," said Mom.
"Maybe Stickybeak could be useful."

So she offered him a snail from the garden.
Stickybeak didn't like it.
Stickybeak didn't want to be useful
if it meant eating snails!

David, who lives next door, has a leash for his dog.
I made a leash for Stickybeak.

The big ducks came to meet Stickybeak.
He ran away.

25

In the botanical gardens,
a guest was making a video of the wedding party.

Dragging his leash, Stickybeak ran quacking past the bride.

Soon the bride's friends and relatives
will see Stickybeak on their video.
They will hear him too.
"Quack!

Quack!

Quack!"

Mom laughed
as we chased Stickybeak through the gardens.

On Sunday night, Mom tried to watch the television news.
"Quack! Quack! Quack!"
Stickybeak wanted to play.

Mom sighed, "I'm glad Stickybeak goes back to class tomorrow."

I haven't told Mom that the class has a pet snake too!

32